The Time Detectives

Terry Deary trained as an actor before turning to writing full time. He has many successful fiction and non-fiction children's books to his name, and is rarely out of the bestseller charts.

Other titles in the series:

The Time Detectives

Book 2

THE PIRATES OF THE DARK PARK

TERRY DEARY

Illustrated by Martin Remphry

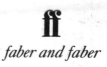

faber and faber

To Alex Paterson. Cheers.

First published in 2000
by Faber and Faber Limited
3 Queen Square London WCIN 3AU

Origination: Miles Kelly Publishing
Printed in Italy

A CIP record for this book
is available from the British Library

ISBN 0-571-20112-1

Contents

The Time Detectives
All about us

These are the files of the toughest team ever to tackle time-crime. We solve mysteries of the past, at last – and fast.

We are the Time Detectives.

My name is Bucket.

Katie Bucket. Commander of the Time Detectives.

And here is my squad. I wrote the secret files myself so you know they're true. Trust me…

Number: TD 001
Name:

Katie Bucket

Appearance:

Gorgeous, beautiful and smart.
The slightly scruffy clothes and messy
hair are just a disguise to fool the
enemy.

Report:

Katie Bucket is the boss,
Grown-ups always make her cross.
She's the Time Detectives' leader.
Cos she's brainy they all need her!

Special skills:

Cunning, brave, quick-thinking. Really
I'm too modest to tell you just how
great I am.

Hobbies:

Playing football, wrestling snakes,
making trouble. (It's a full-time hobby
just being so popular!)

Favourite victim:

Miss Toon our teacher.

Catch-phrase:

"Trust me, I know what I'm doing."

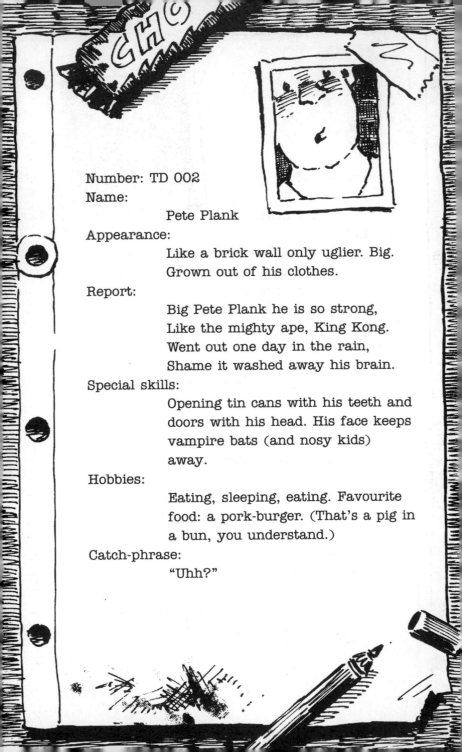

Number: TD 002

Name:

Pete Plank

Appearance:

Like a brick wall only uglier. Big.
Grown out of his clothes.

Report:

Big Pete Plank he is so strong,
Like the mighty ape, King Kong.
Went out one day in the rain,
Shame it washed away his brain.

Special skills:

Opening tin cans with his teeth and
doors with his head. His face keeps
vampire bats (and nosy kids)
away.

Hobbies:

Eating, sleeping, eating. Favourite
food: a pork-burger. (That's a pig in
a bun, you understand.)

Catch-phrase:

"Uhh?"

Number: TD 003

Name:

Gary Grint

Appearance:

A weed with spectacles. Carries more gadgets in his anorak than a moon rocket.

Report:

Gary Grint, computer whiz,
Internetting is his biz.
Knows so much he's awful boring,
Talks till everyone is snoring.

Special skills:

Electronic gadgets, cracking codes, squeezing through small spaces – like letter-boxes.

Hobbies:

Train-spotting, chess, playing the violin (favourite tune: "The dying cat").

Catch-phrase:

"I'll bet you didn't know this!"

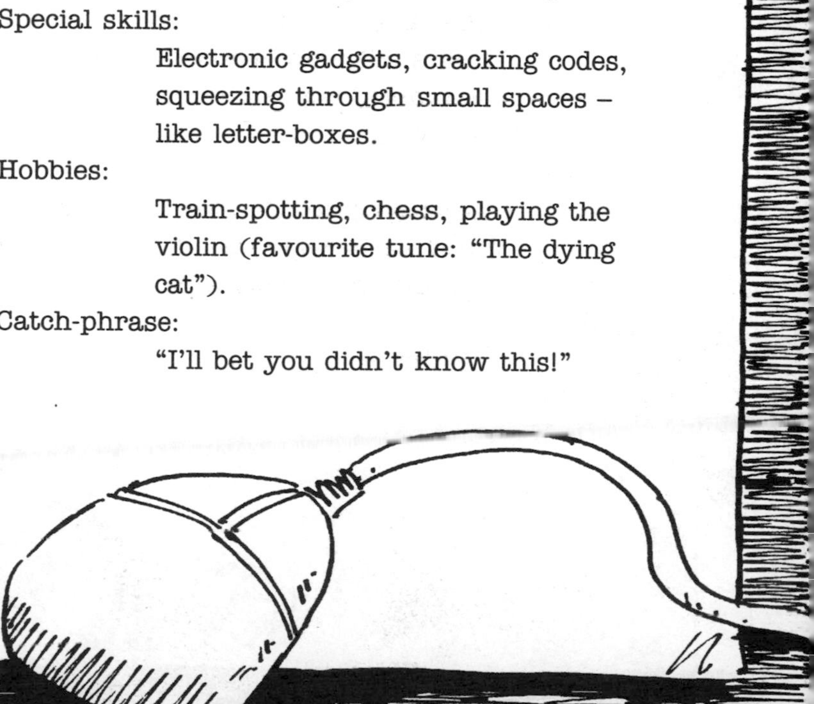

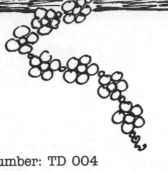

Number: TD 004

Name:

Mabel Tweed

Appearance:

So squeaky clean you could eat your dinner off her shining shoes. She's all posh frocks and white socks.

Report:

Mabel Tweed is so good,
So polite and sweet as pud.
Does her homework neat and quick,
Teacher's pet. She makes me sick!

Special skills:

Creeping, grovelling and being smarmy. I only let the lucky kid join TDs cos her dad's a millionaire.

Hobbies:

Tidying her room, polishing her bike, running errands for adults. Favourite place: at Miss Toon's feet.

Catch-phrase:

"Do excuse me."

Chapter 1
Fish and ships

It all began one October morning when Gary Grint
came in to class with the morning paper, and he
cried, "Cor! Stone the cows! Look at this!"

So, of course we all looked...

The Duckpool Daily News

3 December   55p

RAM-RAIDERS ROBBERY

By our Staff Reporter

Duckpool police are searching for a dangerous gang of ram-raiders who stole a car and used it to batter the front of the High Street chip shop, 'Paddy's Plaice'.

Mr Haddock (49) yesterday.

"I was just serving a nice fat fishcake when a Ford Fiesta flattened the front of me chip shop!" owner Paddy Haddock told our reporter.

The criminals abandoned the car and ran off in the direction of Duckpool Park. One of Paddy's customers, Mrs Molly Macmanus (77) said, "I dropped my purse with the shock. One of the villains picked it up and ran off. It had over £100 in for me Christmas shopping! I heard them shout out, 'We'll be back! And next time we'll hit the right target!'"

The scene of the crime.

Police are baffled. Inspector Norse says, "We are not sure just what they were aiming at. What was their right target?" Meanwhile Paddy Haddock's neighbours, from The Jolly Gem Jewellery Shop and The Coin Collectors Cabin, helped the flustered fish-seller to sweep up the glass.

The car was later reported stolen. The car owner, Police Inspector Norman Norse, said he did not want to be named. It seems he had left his keys in the car which was parked outside Duckpool police station.

Inspector Norse, who does not want to be named, said, "The police are searching the town for two short men with dirty hand-kerchiefs over their mouths as masks. We will catch these highway robbers if it's the last thing we do! We can't have dangerously deadly dodgem cars driving round demolishing Duckpool!"

Inspector Norse

The Duckpool Association of Fish Traders (D.A.F.T.) announced a thousand-pound reward for information leading to the capture of the villains.

Pete Plank scratched his large head. "What's a ram-raider, Katie?" he asked me.

"Well, you know what a ram is?" I asked him.

"Yeah!" he cried, excited. "A ram's a daddy sheep! And radar's what they use to spot aeroplanes! So ram radars go round trying to spot daddy sheep!" he looked pleased with himself. Then he frowned. "What do they do that for, Katie? What do they do with the rams when they find them? Do they take them to the chip shop for supper?"

I smiled at him and patted his brick-thick skull. "Pete..."

"Yes, Katie?"

"Shut up."

"Yes, Katie."

Just then our class teacher, Miss Toon, walked into the room and asked what we were reading. "About that raid on the chip shop last night!" Gary told her. "It's the most exciting thing in Duckpool since... since..."

"Since Queen Victoria came to visit the town but got lost and went to Blackpool by mistake," I said. It was true. Duckpool is as dull as Pete Plank's shirt collars.

The teacher nodded and muttered, "They're just modern-day pirates."

Pete gasped, "And are these pilots flying the planes with the radars?"

Miss Toon blinked. "I said 'pirates', Pete, not 'pilots'. You know... sailors who went around attacking ships."

"Paddy's Plaice wasn't attacked by a ship," Pete argued.

"No, Pete," Miss Toon said patiently. "I meant that these robbers are modern-day pirates – they just use cars instead of ships." She moved to her cupboard and pulled out a folder. "Two of my pupils did a project on pirates last year. This is what they wrote about them before they started their project. Not everything they wrote was right. I'd like you to have a look at the list."

She pushed a sheet of notepaper towards us...

DUCKPOOL EDUCATIONAL TRUST

HISTORY WORKSHEET

Pirates

1 cruel and ruthless men   ——

2 parrots   ——

3 Spanish gold and jewels   ——

4 maps of buried treasure   ——

5 fine clothes, black beards
   and curly wigs   ——

6 wooden legs and eye-patches ——

7 skull-and-crossbone flags   ——

8 marooning shipmates on
   desert islands   ——

9 walking the plank   ——

10 a crocodile that's swallowed
    a clock   ——

"How many of those ten things are true?" she asked. "And how many are just stories?"

"I don't know, Miss Toon," I said wearily. "How many are true and how many are stories?"

"I think you should turn into Time Detectives and find that out for yourself. I'm just a teacher. I don't know everything!" she said with a crafty smile. I just knew she was going to say that. It's her sly way of getting us to work. "But I'll give you a clue," she smiled.

"You're the kindest teacher in the whole of this classroom," I told her. "What's the clue?"

"The two who wrote that had clearly read the book *Peter Pan*. That's where they got 9 and 10 from! The croc and the clock were just part of the story. And real pirates never ever made their victims walk the plank. Why waste the time? They just cut them up and threw them overboard!"

I took the list and marked the last two notes...

DUCKPOOL EDUCATIONAL TRUST

HISTORY WORKSHEET

Pirates

1 cruel and ruthless men ——

2 parrots ——

3 Spanish gold and jewels ——

4 maps of buried treasure ——

5 fine clothes, black beards
   and curly wigs ——

6 wooden legs and eye-patches ——

7 skull-and-crossbone flags ——

8 marooning shipmates on
   desert islands ——

9 walking the plank

10 a crocodile that's swallowed
   a clock ✗

I'd have left the rest to our computer expert Gary Grint, but Miss Toon said something interesting. "If you understand how pirates in history lived then you may understand a little more about today's ram-raiders. Why do they do it? And how can they be so cruel?"

"Ramming a chip shop is cruel?" Gary laughed.

"No – but stealing an old lady's purse is pretty rotten," Pete said.

"I was thinking of the cruelty of the pirates of old," Miss Toon said. "Look at this report by a young woman who was captured by pirates," she said and spread a photograph of an old letter in front of us. "Some Cuban pirates captured the English ship *Eliza Ann*. A woman called Lucretia Parker wrote to her brother to tell the tale of what happened to the crew."

We read it with horror...

First they took off all of the crew's clothes except their shirts and trousers. Then they attacked them with swords, knives and axes. They were as ferocious as cannibals. They ignored pleas for mercy as the crew begged the murderers to spare their lives.

Our Captain Smith tried to win the pirates' pity by telling them of his wife and three small children. But he was pleading with monsters who have no human feelings. After receiving a heavy blow from an axe he snapped the cords he was bound with and, trying to escape, he was met by another of the ruffians who plunged a knife into his heart.

I was standing near him at the time and was covered with his blood. On receiving the wound he gave a single groan and fell, lifeless, at my feet. Dear brother, I don't need to paint a picture of my feelings at that awful moment!

"How did she escape?" Gary gasped.

"A British warship appeared before they could turn on Lucretia. The pirates abandoned the *Eliza Ann* and she was saved. They were arrested later in Jamaica. Lucretia Parker identified them and had the pleasure of watching them hang," Miss Toon said with a grim smile.

She left the room to collect the register and I turned to my Time Detectives team. "How about it, Time Tecs? We can find out about pirates, solve the crime…"

"And get the Fish Traders' thousand pounds!" Gary grinned.

Pete sniffed. "I like fish, Katie, but I don't think I could eat a thousand pounds of the stuff."

I sighed. "Pete."

"Yes, Katie?"

"Shut up."

"Yes, Katie."

Chapter 2
The wild women

I went off to read the book that Miss Toon said was the first book written about pirates. *A General History Of The Robberies And Murders Of The Most Notorious Pirates*, by Captain Charles Johnson. And the man that wrote it probably knew a lot of the pirates he was writing about. "It's what we call in history a 'primary' source," Miss Toon explained. "Primary means 'first' – so you're often getting first-hand information."

"So it's dead right!" I nodded.

"No – Johnson might have been repeating old stories the pirates told him. And some of the pirates may have added bits to their stories to make them sound better!" she said, just to confuse me.

"So primary sources aren't always true?" I asked. She shook her head. "So how can we tell what's true?"

"Good historians use facts – but they also use a bit of common sense," she said.

"Common sense and primary sources," I said.

Pete said, "I prefer tomato sauces." I looked at him. He shrugged. "I know, Katie. Shut up?"

Miss Toon looked at him through her long, dark lashes. "No, Pete. You may not be the best reader in the class, and some of these books may be a bit difficult for you. But the Time Detectives need something very important that you can give them."

"What? Me?" he said, and blushed.

"Yes, Pete. You have common sense," she told him. "Let Katie read the books and let Gary search the internet. But you ask the questions. You're good at that!"

"Am I?"

"You are."

Gary and I were getting a bit fed up with this lovey-dovey stuff so Gary said, "I'll bet you didn't know this! Get your common sense around this, Pete," and he opened the Johnson book and read him the tale of Mary and Anne...

Once, in England, a baby girl was born to a Mrs Read. The mother named the child Mary. But the baby girl's father deserted her and the mother had no money to feed Mary and her older child, Jim. Then Jim died. And Mrs Read brought Mary up as the son she had lost. Mary grew up dressed as a boy and behaving like a boy.

When she was 13 years old Mary became a footman to a French lady, but she hated the life of a servant so she joined the crew of a warship. There were many boys on board ships in those days and a young woman like Mary could dress in men's jackets and trousers.

Mary left the navy for a while and she served as a soldier in Holland and fought bravely in many battles. She married a soldier when the war was over and they opened a tavern called The Three Horseshoes.

υ υ υ

Her husband died, and Mary joined the army once again. When her ship set sail for the West Indies it was attacked by pirates and she was captured. Mary joined the pirate crew led by a man called Calico Jack. To Mary's surprise she found there was already a woman pirate on the ship – Calico Jack's wife, Anne Bonny.

Anne had been brought up as a boy in Ireland. She married a poor sailor and her father drove Anne from his house. She was forced to live with the sailor in the West Indies. That's where she met Calico Jack, the pirate, who stole her from her husband and turned her into a pirate.

So Mary Read and Anne Bonny roved the seas and robbed traders. But they were finally caught and brought to trial by the British navy. Calico Jack and his crew were hanged. Jack's body was put in a cage and hung up at Deadman's Cay for all to see.

Then Mary and Anne were sent for trial. One of the British sailors who arrested them said the women were waving pistols, swearing and fighting as hard as any of the men. The judge decided they should hang too. But Mary and Anne said they were expecting babies. The law of the day said they had to be sent to prison instead and they were. Mary died of a fever in her jail soon after. Anne survived but no-one is sure what happened to her and her baby afterwards.

"Well, Pete?" I asked.

"Well!" he said. "Just goes to show... we were wrong about the very first thing on our pirate list! We said pirates were cruel and toothless men..."

"Ruthless, Pete. Ruthless."

"Uhh? Yeah. Well – anyway. There were ruel and cruthless women too!" I put a cross against number one on Miss Toon's list.

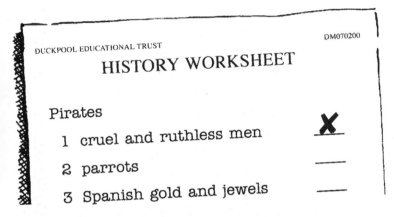

DUCKPOOL EDUCATIONAL TRUST

DM070200

HISTORY WORKSHEET

Pirates

1 cruel and ruthless men   ✗

2 parrots   ____

3 Spanish gold and jewels   ____

"Well, Pete? Use your common sense. Is that story about Mary and Anne true?"

But he wasn't listening. He was looking at the newspaper. "Those rammy radar people could be women," he muttered.

"What?"

"Just cos someone pinches a car and attacks a chip shop doesn't mean they're men," he said. "Anne and Mary weren't."

I looked at him and said, "Thanks Planks! Good thinking! The police are looking for two men. What if they're wrong?"

"We should tell them," Pete said.

"Nah! They wouldn't believe us."

"So we'll just let them get away with it?"

"No, Pete. We crack the crime ourselves! We become detectives!"

"We become pirates!" Gary said.

I thought Gary was potty. He sits there, tapping away at his computer and he's in a world of his own. Behind his round, owl-glasses his eyes were sparkling. "Explain!" I commanded.

"There's an old saying," he said. "Set a thief to catch a thief!"

"Uhh?" Pete frowned. "You want us to become thieves?"

"Exactly!" Gary cried, and I knew he'd flipped.

Chapter 3

The ram-raiding pirate

Gary showed us what he'd been studying on his computer. "When the British navy wanted to get rid of pirates around Jamaica, who do you think they appointed as the chief pirate-catcher?"

Gary had the answer on the screen of his laptop computer, not in his head. I pulled it away from him to have a look...

Sir Henry MORGAN

Born in Wales about 1635

Joined the British army and helped capture Jamaica from the Spanish.

Became a 'privateer' – that is a pirate who attacks foreign ships for his king.

By the age of 32 he was leader of the pirates in the West Indies, attacking Spanish treasure ships and Spanish towns in Central America.

In 1668 Morgan sailed to the Spanish treasure port of Portobello. The guns on the town's fortress pointed out to sea – aimed at any ships sailing towards the town. So Morgan came ashore up the coast and attacked from the land. He captured the town and its fort. The Spanish were forced to pay Britain 350,000 pesos to get their town back.

The next year he led an attack on other Spanish towns. But this time Morgan was faced with a huge Spanish galleon, blocking his escape. He took a stolen Spanish trading-ship and packed it with barrels of gunpowder. He disguised it as a warship with logs for cannon and dummies for sailors and a few of his privateers sailed it towards the mighty galleon. As the stolen trading-ship crashed into the galleon the privateers lit the fuses and escaped on a canoe. The trading-ship exploded, the galleon was destroyed and Morgan's little fleet escaped the Spanish trap.

Henry Morgan went on to be the governor of Jamaica. The pirate had become a pirate-catcher.

"See!" Gary said. "Miss Toon was right. Pirates were a sort of early ram-raider. They used stolen ships to batter their way through the enemy the way modern thieves use stolen cars."

"But they didn't batter their way into chip shops," Pete grunted.

I was just about to say, "Don't be stupid!" when I remembered what Miss Toon had said about his common sense. "You're right, Pete."

"Uhh? I am?"

"Yeah! If we can find out what they were up to we may be able to solve the crime and catch the crooks!"

Pete brightened. "Where do we start, Katie?"

"We question the witnesses and search the crime scene, of course. Trust me. I know what I'm doing."

"What about our pirate work?" Pete asked.

That reminded me of the list. Henry Morgan attacked Spanish treasure ships...

Pirates

1 cruel and ruthless men   **X**

2 parrots   **✓**

3 Spanish gold and jewels   **✓**

4 maps of buried treasure   —

Then I turned back to Pete. "This is pirate work – Miss Toon said the car thieves were pirates! We can learn about historical pirates at the same time – and get ourselves a thousand pound reward!"

"I've been trying to tell you," Gary said wearily.

"We have to become pirates like Henry Morgan. When the British were attacked by Spanish pirates then they asked Henry Morgan to defend them! Look, here's the order," he said, showing us the computer screen...

1st August 1670
The Council Of Jamaica agrees that Admiral Henry Morgan is ordered to attack, seize and destroy all the enemy ships that come within his reach. He may also land on enemy country to take and destroy anything that could threaten the peace of Jamaica.

"The best person to beat a pirate is... another pirate!" Gary said.

I scratched my head. "So, you're saying we have to plan a ram-raid to understand the ram-raiders?"

"That is exactly what I'm saying," Gary said. "But you have to be careful. Henry Morgan attacked the Spanish city of Panama – then he was arrested by the British for doing what he was told."

"Uhh? That's not fair," Pete said.

"They soon forgave him and King Charles knighted Morgan. Then he was sent back to Jamaica as governor. So it worked out all right in the end."

"We may have to break a few laws ourselves," I said. "But if we catch the villains it'll work all right for us too," I decided. I scribbled a note for Miss Toon...

1. Dear Miss Toon
Pete Plank and Katie Bucket have gone to Duckpool to do some piratical research and to attack, seize and destroy the enemy.
Love
    Katie

Pete followed me through the door. "I still say we'll never eat a thousand pounds of fish."

Chapter 4
The four-legged purring parrot

Pete, Gary and I walked down the corridor quickly. We'd left the note for Miss Toon but we didn't really want to explain to her face. She might go on about cruel and ruthless robbers turning on us with axes and cutlasses when we caught them. Teachers can be a bit fussy like that.

We slipped past the room of Mr 'Potty' Potterton, our headteacher. The door out to the street creaked like Potty's knees when he climbed onto the stage to take assembly. I waved Pete and Gary out and was just about to follow them when a voice said, "Do excuse me! But where do you three think you're off to?"

I groaned. I turned to look at the cleanest girl in Duckpool. Her shoes were so shiny they dazzled sparrows on sunny days and made them fly into telegraph poles. Mabel Tweed! "What do you want, weedy Tweedy?" I asked.

"I want to know where you're going," she demanded. "And does Miss Toon know you are leaving school?"

"I left her a note," I said.

Mabel smirked on her apple-cheeked face. "I thought so, you somewhat scruffy girl. You're off on one of your Time Detective adventures, aren't you?" she asked, and before I could answer she went on, "Well, I'm coming with you. I've decided that I'm a Time Detective too. Daddy's a millionaire, you know."

She flounced past me in her frilled dress and, before I could stop her, she had the whole story from Gary and Pete. "So, we're going to become pirates, are we? Then the first thing I need is a parrot on my shoulder!"

"That's only in films and books, you understand," I sneered. "Tell her, Gary."

But Mabel had run off to her house to collect a parrot. She warned us to wait – or she'd go back to school and tell Miss Toon. The little creep.

Gary was looking through the folder Miss Toon had given us. His eyebrows rose above the rims of his spectacles. "I'll bet you didn't know this!"

"No – but I'll bet you're going to tell us," I said.

"In the book, *Treasure Island*, the villainous Long John Silver has a parrot called Captain Flint."

"And a wooden leg called Captain Splint," I muttered to Pete.

"There have been at least five films and dozens of stage plays based on *Treasure Island*, and they all have the parrot. That's where people like Mabel get the idea from."

"Gary," I said, "I could have guessed that myself. Can you please just tell her that real pirates never had parrots so she can get the daft idea out of her head!"

"That's what I'm trying to tell you! Look!"

He pulled a small pocket book out of his anorak and showed us...

DID YOU KNOW...

SAILORS who went to South America often caught parrots as souvenirs. They were easy to look after on board ship and they could be sold for a good price when the sailors arrived back in Europe. They made popular pets because they could be taught how to talk. A 1717 advert in 'The Post Man' newspaper said:

"For sale: parakeets which talk English, Dutch, French and Spanish.
They will whistle when you command them.
Very tame and pretty."

So pirates, like any other sailor, would often be seen with a parrot.

Mabel came back five minutes later. She was riding a glittering bicycle. It was gleaming gold with silver spokes. But it wasn't the bike that caught our eye. Pete gasped, Gary blinked and I laughed. "What's that?" I hooted, pointing to the black thing on her shoulder.

"My Minnie. She's my parrot," Mabel said.

"I've never seen a parrot with black fur and four legs," poor puzzled Pete said. "Does it talk?"

"No, but it purrs, Pete," I told him.

"A purring parrot?"

"Pete – it's a cat," I explained.

"But Mabel said..."

"Mabel is pretending," I said. "She seems to think this is some kind of game." I turned on her. "Well, it's not a game, weedy Tweedy. It's for real. We want that thousand pound reward."

Mabel rode ahead of us to the row of shops where the ram-raid had happened.

As we walked I took out my copy of Miss Toon's list and put a tick against number 2.

Pirates

   1 cruel and ruthless men   ✗

   2 parrots   ✓

   3 Spanish gold and jewels   ✓

   4 maps of buried treasure   —

Paddy's Plaice was repaired now and workmen were sweeping up the last of the broken glass.

A man stood by the chip-shop door with thin hair combed from ear to ear to cover his baldness. "Do excuse me, sweeper-chappie, my good man," Mabel was saying when we got there. "Are you Mr Plaice?"

"No, to be sure, I'm Paddy and this is my place."

"Oh… it's the same thing, really," said Mabel, sniffily. "We're working on a magazine for Duckpool Primary, and so we thought we might be able to interview you."

"About me fish or me chips?" Paddy asked and smoothed his hair in place as if we were going to take his photo.

"About your robbery," I said.

"Well, sure, it wasn't me that was robbed. It was old Mrs Macmanus," Paddy explained.

"Has anyone found her purse?" Mabel asked.

"Now it's strange you should ask that. Someone handed it to me just this morning. They didn't know where she lives but they knew she'd be in for her cod tonight," the chip-shop owner said.

"Was the purse empty?" I asked.

"Empty of her money," he said. "But here's a funny thing," he said, reaching into his pocket. "There was this scrap of paper inside."

He opened the folded paper and handed it to us. It was drawn in ball-point pen on a piece of paper torn from a school book. "A clue!" Mabel said.

"Can we take it?" I asked.

"Certainly not! That's the property of Mrs Macmanus!" the man said.

I was desperate to hold on to this vital clue because I knew what it was... it was a map! A map of an island with three trees and a cross marked in the middle of them. This was where the raiders had buried their treasure until the fuss died down.

But how would I get to hold on to the map? My brain hurt. Then, Pete came up with the answer. "Here, Mabel? Where's your parrot?"

"What? Minnie?" she asked and looked at her shoulder. The four-legged parrot had hopped it. "Oh, my darling little Minnie!" she cried.

"It's just that there's a black parrot, just like
yours, pinching the fish off the table in the shop!"
Pete said.

We looked through the new glass window into the
shop. Sure enough, there was Minnie tucking into a
tasty piece of haddock. The shop-owner gave a roar
of rage and rushed into his shop. "How did that cat
get in here!"

He waved a filleting knife and Minnie raced out
with the fish in her mouth – or do I mean her beak?
Paddy bent to pick up the fish that she'd scattered on
the floor. This was our chance. "Run for it!" I cried
and headed down the road towards the park.

Mabel leapt onto her golden cycle and rode
alongside us. "Do excuse me, Katie Bucket, but
you've just stolen that map! I ought to report you."

"Yeah…" I panted. "And your parrot's just stolen Paddy's fish. I ought to report her. She'll be locked away in a cage for life and they'll throw away her perch!" We were in the shelter of the bushes at the entrance to the park. We stopped running and Mabel braked to a halt. "Well?" I asked her.

She stuck her little button nose in the air and shook her ringlets. "Well… perhaps we'll just look at the paper and return it to the old lady later."

"Oooh!" Pete whispered. "We're real thieves now!"

Chapter 5
Buried treasure and a park pond

We walked down the park paths that twisted through bare bushes and muddy beds of dead flowers. At last we reached the pond in the middle. A row of rowing-boats rocked in the choppy water and clanked the chains that locked them to rings on the shore. I imagined chains like that around my legs when they locked me in prison for fish theft and stealing from an old lady's purse.

"Yeah, Pete," I said. "We're criminals now. The only way to save ourselves is to catch the real thieves and find the old lady's money."

"We have the pirates' treasure map!" Gary said. For some reason we were speaking in whispers.

"Uhh?" Pete gasped. "Have we?"

"Yes, Pete!" I explained. "That's why I took it. They stole the money and then they hid it."

"Just like real pirates!" Pete said.

But Gary looked at his computer and shook his head. "I'll bet you didn't know this! Real pirates never drew treasure maps," he said. "They stole stuff and sold it. Then they spent the money in pirate taverns and had to go back and steal more stuff. No pirate in his right mind would bury money!"

"Long John Silver did," Mabel argued and stroked the purring parrot that was back on her shoulder, licking its fishy beak.

Gary sighed. "*Treasure Island* is just make-believe, Mabel."

"So no-one buried treasure and drew a map?" I asked and crossed it off my list...

Pirates

1 cruel and ruthless men

2 parrots

3 Spanish gold and jewels

4 maps of buried treasure

5 fine clothes, black beards
and curly wigs

"The idea of buried treasure comes from two places. One was Treasure Island. But the map came before the story!" Gary explained. "The writer was a man called Robert Louis Stevenson. He was on holiday in Scotland and it was really pouring with rain. He had his step-son, Lloyd, with him and the boy was bored."

"No telly," I nodded.

"Couldn't they afford one?" Pete asked.

"It hadn't been invented, you large boy with a small brain," Mabel snapped.

"Anyway," Gary went on. The boy had a box of paints and one afternoon his step-father joined him. Look ... Lloyd wrote about it when he grew up ..."

Robert Louis Stevenson sat beside me and began sharing my paints. He decided to paint the map of an imagined island. Then he took a pen and began adding the names of the hills and the bays. I shall never forget the thrill of Skeleton Island, Spyglass Hill, or the way my heart was stirred at the sight of the three red crosses. And the greatest thrill of all when he wrote the words "Treasure Island" at the top right-hand corner!

And he seemed to know so much about it too – the pirates, the buried treasure, the man who had been marooned on the island.

In three days he had written three chapters and he read each one to the family. We all added our own ideas. It was my idea that there should be no women in this story. Grandpa came up with a list of the things in Billy Bones' sea chest and with the scene where Jim Hawkins hides in the apple barrel.

The dreadful Scottish weather made my step-father ill so the book wasn't finished until we went on holiday to Switzerland and he recovered. Of course it became hugely popular and we were delighted to hear that the Prime Minister, Mr Gladstone, stayed up until two in the morning to finish the story.

This great book was written for boys but it is as popular with adults as with children. And it all started with that painting of a map on a wet afternoon.

"He even pinched the famous song from a book called *At Last*," Gary told us.

"What song?" Pete asked.

"You know...

Fifteen men on the Dead Man's Chest!
Yo, ho, ho, and a bottle of rum!" ✗

I was disappointed. "So, you're saying that pirates never buried their treasure?"

"I said they never drew treasure maps. There are just a few famous cases of buried treasure... but I'm not sure that they'd help us," Gary said, squinting at the screen of his computer. I looked over his shoulder...

BURIED PIRATE TREASURE

1   Sir Francis Drake. In 1571 Drake landed near the Spanish treasure port of Nombre de Dios in America and hid by the road through the forest. This was the road where the gold arrived at the port.

Drake's men attacked a mule train carrying Spanish gold. His ships were a few miles away along the coast and there was too much treasure to carry. So Drake's men buried about fifteen tons of silver in the gravel at the river's edge. They carried off what they could.

The Spanish caught some of the pirates and forced them to show where the gold was hidden before they beheaded them. By the time Drake returned most of the treasure had been dug up.

"So they hid it because there was too much to carry away?" I said. "Nah, you're right, Gary, that doesn't help us. Mrs Macmanus's money wasn't too heavy. What else have you got?"

We looked at the screen...

BURIED PIRATE TREASURE

2 Captain William Kidd. In 1698 Captain Kidd took a rich ship in the Indian Ocean. He sailed to the West Indies where he discovered the British navy were hunting him as a pirate. He switched ships and went to New York where he hoped his powerful friends would save him. In fact his powerful friends had the pirate arrested and sent to London for trial. He was hanged. Many people believe he left the West Indies with £400,000 of treasure. When he was arrested he had only about £14,000. They believe he buried most of the treasure so that the law wouldn't find it. To this day people try searching for Captain Kidd's treasure.

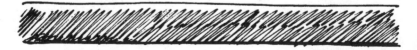

I nodded. "That's possible. Our thieves want to come back for it when they think the robbery's been forgotten."

"Or maybe," Gary said, "The thieves don't want to be found with £100 on them. The law will get suspicious! There's one more case of buried treasure," Gary muttered, and he showed us...

BURIED PIRATE TREASURE

3 Captain Stratton. In 1720 the captain stopped his ship before he reached Yorktown harbour in America. He unloaded six bags of silver coins and six chests of treasure. Captain Stratton had traded with pirates for the silver and didn't want to be caught with it on board his ship. He sailed into Yorktown but one of his crew betrayed Stratton and he was arrested. The treasure was evidence and Stratton didn't want to be seen with it.

Mabel Tweed sniffed. "Do excuse me, but that's nonsense. My daddy's a millionaire. My daddy always has at least £100 in his pocket. Nothing suspicious about having £100 on you."

I was going to say something very rude about Mabel's dad but, luckily, Pete Plank spoke up. "Well, my dad's a car mechanic and he's never had £100 in his pocket."

"Brilliant, Pete!" I cried. "That's it! We're looking for someone poor. Someone who wouldn't usually have £100. They'd have to hide it or the police would be suspicious!"

"Like my dad?" Pete asked, worried.

"Or you... or me or Gary!" I said.

"Yeah... but we're just kids," Pete said. "The thieves weren't kids."

I looked at him with wonder. I would have kissed him – but I didn't want to dirty my lips. "How do we know? Look at the report..."

Inspector Norse, who does not want to be named, said, "The police are searching the town for two short men with dirty handkerchiefs over their mouths as masks. We will catch the highway robbers

The Du of Fish T announce reward fo ing to the lains.

"Two short men... or kids. That explains why they drove so badly!"

"I'm a kid," Pete said. "And I drive quite well. My dad taught me on the waste ground behind his garage."

"Personally I would use Daddy's chauffeur," Mabel said.

"Shut up, you two," I said. "Let's imagine we are two poor kids. We set off to do a pirate attack to make some Christmas money. Let's plan it..."

Chapter 6
Plotting in the dark park

A bell rang through the gloomy park. "Closing time," I said and rose stiffly to my feet.

It was getting colder now and the boats were starting to freeze in to the shallow water at the edge of the park pond. Minnie was testing it with her paw to see if she could get over the ice to those ducks on a little island in the middle. It was time for some warming action.

Mabel Tweed pulled on thick, fur-lined gloves and wrinkled her little nose that was turning red. "Well, Katie Bucket. Where do we start?"

"I'm glad you asked me that," I said.

"I'm glad you're glad," she said.

"I'm glad you're glad I'm glad," I said.

"I'm glad you're... oh, stop it, Katie. Tell me the answer!" she snapped and wheeled her golden bike alongside me.

"Let's get out of the park before they lock us in," I told the Time Detectives. I was still stalling for time. We walked towards the park gate that led out to the Duckpool sea front. The out-door swimming-pool was deserted, its high diving-board rearing up like the scaffold you draw on paper when you play hangman.

As we reached the gate the park-keeper was sitting in a small cabin, listening to the radio...

"And this is the four o'clock news from Duckpool FM Radio. First, the latest report on the ram-raid at Paddy's Plaice chip shop. Police have reported that four small criminals – two male and two female - approached the scene of the crime and made off with a vital clue – a treasure map. They are believed to be members of the gang that ram-raided the shop last night.

"That's us!" Pete gasped before Gary slapped a hand over his babbling mouth.

The villains are described as ugly and desperate. The public are warned that these criminals are dangerous and not to approach them but to call their nearest police station. They are also carrying a large black beast, a bit like a four-legged vulture, on the shoulder of the ugliest one... the public are being warned to keep their dogs indoors.

"Oh, I say!" Mabel exclaimed. "They mean my little Minnie! But she isn't on the shoulder of the ugliest one... she's on my shoulder!"

These young tearaways were in possession of a golden bicycle – obviously the loot from an earlier raid. The public are being warned to keep their bikes indoors. The police are searching Duckpool with dogs, but a dog-handler said, "We have no leads."

The park-keeper gave a short laugh. "The police dogs'll run away if they have no leads!" He switched off the radio and came to the door of his hut.

He was a thin, round-shouldered man in a worn navy overcoat and a battered navy cap with a tarnished badge on the front. He tapped the peak. "Good evening," he said. "Hurry on home before it gets dark. There's a bunch of vicious kids around!"

"Thank you, Mr... er..." Mabel said.

"Mr Dark – Dark of the Park they call me. Nice bike," he sighed.

"It's gold-plated, don't you know. Daddy's a millionaire."

He shook his head. "I'd be glad of any sort of bike. Paper-plate would do."

"You can't get paper-plate," Mabel snapped.

"We use paper plates on picnics," Pete Plank said brightly. Mabel ignored him.

"You don't need a bike to ride around this little park?" Mabel sneered at the keeper.

He shook his head miserably. "No, Miss. I meant as a Christmas present for the kids. Parkkeepers don't get paid much, you know. And I don't think I can afford one bike for the kids, never mind two."

"For two kids?" I asked.

"Twins," he nodded and wiped away a drop of water that dripped from the end of his cold, thin nose.

He led us out of the dark park, shut the gates with a clang and fastened a chain around them. "Poor bloke," I muttered as we walked back towards the town centre. At least, three of us walked and one rode.

"Look, Katie Bucket," Mabel said briskly. "I asked you where a pirate raid would start. You haven't given me an answer yet."

I opened and closed my mouth like a goldfish while Pete and Mabel looked at me. It was Gary who came to my rescue. "Research," he said.

Mabel blinked. "That's what we do for history," she said.

"And it's what the best pirates did," Gary explained. He stepped under a street lamp that was flickering on and pulled a sheet of crumpled paper from his pocket. "I took this out of Miss Toon's file before we left school," he said. "Someone from Miss Toon's class last year made these notes..."

From Page 15 of "The World Encompassed"
written by Sir Francis Drake

"And our spy did inform us that the treasure of Lima was on its way to Panama on a train of fourteen mules. The treasurer and his family would ride on four of the mules. Eight would be carrying gold and two larger ones at the back would carry the food. We were able to wait by the roadside where we knew they would pass that evening. My men wore their shirts outside their clothes so we would know one another in the darkness. We split into two parties, mine to take the leading mules and John Oxenham's to take the rear. It would have been foolish to have had my two groups at each side of the road since then we would have been shooting towards each other, if shooting was what was needed."

"So Drake used spies," I told Mabel. "See? Research."

"I think Drake used an escaped slave to get the details about the treasure," Gary said.

"And who did the research before the raid on Paddy's Plaice?" Mabel asked. "An escaped slave?"

Gary pushed a second piece of paper in front of her...

Page 37 "Sir Francis Drake Revived" – probably written by Sir Francis Drake.

"Before the attack on Nombre de Dios I decided to spy out the town for myself. I entered the town disguised as a merchant and stayed there a week, drawing a map of the important parts. I marked down where the Spanish guns were that defended the town and where the army camp was. I noted where the store-houses for the silver and gold were built and where my men could land without being seen by the guards. I drew a map of the streets for my men so they knew their way to the treasure houses and the ways back to the safety of our ships.

"We would do the spying for ourselves, Mabel – just the way Drake did," I said.

"Do excuse me, rather silly Time Detective, but we'd be spotted. The whole of Duckpool is looking out for us! We're wanted criminals!" Mabel told me.

I put a hand on Mabel's golden bike and stopped her. "We'd be in disguise – for a start you can leave that bike behind... not to mention that cat!"

"It's a parrot," she sniffed. "And I can't leave my bike because I'd have to walk. I'm the mayor's daughter, you know. I can't be seen tramping the streets!"

I groaned. "Mabel. After tea we will meet on the corner of the street. We will all be in disguise. If you have that bike then I will disguise it by placing it in the path of the first passing bus." She looked shocked and annoyed but I went on. "And if the parrot is with you it will be in the saddle-bag when the bus mashes the miaow out of it. Understand?"

"You are a cruel and ruthless person," she muttered.

"Then I'll make a good pirate, won't I?" I grinned. I turned to the gang who were goggling at me. "Meet at the corner. Six o'clock. All right?"

"Aye, aye, captain," Gary said.

Chapter 7
A golden leg and
a golden hoard

I didn't have much time for tea. I was too busy
preparing my disguise.

As I'd munched my way through my beans on
toast that tea-time I'd watched a television
programme. It was all about pirates and how to
disguise yourself as one. They said pirates often
wore the fine clothes and wigs they stole from rich
victims. And the pirate Blackbeard really did have a
black beard!

I copied the instructions. First I took a large spotted handkerchief and tied it around my head, then I made an eye-patch out of black cardboard and fastened it over one eye. I blacked out a couple of teeth and strapped a wooden chair-leg on to my knee.

I made a pirate coat, from my school coat with silver foil wrapped round the buttons. Now no-one would recognise me as Katie Bucket. Everyone would think I was on my way to a fancy-dress party.

The television programme also showed how to make a pirate costume and then it went on about wooden legs...

...but he didn't have a wooden leg. He got around on crutches!

If you're going to be a pirate you could have a wooden leg and be quite accurate. Yeah! How about that?

During ship battles it wasn't unusual for a seaman to lose a leg – or an arm... or even a head! Of course they didn't replace them with wooden heads! Ho! Ho!

A shattered leg could be removed with the ship's saw! And nothing to kill the pain! Ouchy! Ouchy!

The stump would be sealed with a red-hot iron tool like an axe! Yeuchy sizzle! Yeuchy sizzle!

It was the popular 1700s painter Rowlandson who showed wounded sailors balancing on wooden legs! Amazing, eh?

Here's one I made earlier from an old chair-leg. Don't try this at home, kids! Enjoy that party!

I had checked Miss Toon's list...

3 ᴚpᴀᴀᴀᴀ ᴦᴏᴀᴀᴀᴀᴀᴀ ᴇ   ✗
4 maps of buried treasure   ✗
5 fine clothes, black beards and curly wigs   ✔
6 wooden legs and eye-patches   ✔
7 skull-and-cross bone flags   —
8 mᴀᴦᴏᴏning shipᴛᴀᴀtes on

I hobbled down the stairs on my wooden leg and called through the kitchen door, "Off to Gary Grint's house to do some homework, Mum!"

Before she could answer there was a tremendous crash and a howl of agony from Dad. "Ooooh! Me back!" he wailed.

"What's wrong, pet?" I heard Mum ask.

"The chair – the kitchen chair – it just collapsed as soon as I sat on it. Ooooh! Me back! Ooooh! Me bum!"

There was a clattering and a splintering as if someone was picking up wooden pieces. I limped quietly towards the front door. "Eeeeh! That's funny," Mum was saying. "I can only find three chair-legs – somebody's sawn off the other one and pinched it!"

I opened the door – and hopped it.

Well, my need was greater than Dad's. When I reached the street corner I was amazed to see three pirates waiting for me – all dressed the same as I was!

"You saw that programme on telly too then, Katie?" Gary asked.

"Me too," Pete said.

Of course Mabel's leg was carefully carved and covered in gold leaf. "I got this from the mayor's chair in the Town Hall. Daddy won't be needing it till the Grand Christmas Draw tonight at eight o'clock," she explained.

"What if we're late?" I groaned. "The leg of the mayor's chair won't be there!"

"Don't care!" she sniffed. "Anyway. He can't go to the Town Hall without the mayor's car and he doesn't have it. I ordered the driver to bring me here," she said and nodded to the side-street where the glittering limousine waited.

"Mabel! This is a secret meeting," I said angrily and my breath smoked like a pirate's pipe in the freezing air.

"You said I couldn't bring my bicycle. Surely you didn't expect me to walk!"

I shook my head helplessly and hard... so hard I almost fell off my wooden leg. "Let's look at the shop and see how the raiders must have planned it," I said and we hobbled across the road to Paddy's Plaice. Paddy's customers gave us curious looks as four pirates stared in at the new window.

"Why rob a chip shop?" Gary wondered.

"Don't know," I sighed.

"Don't know," Mabel sighed.

"What if we're late?" I groaned. "The leg of the mayor's chair won't be there!"

"Don't care!" she sniffed. "Anyway. He can't go to the Town Hall without the Mayor's car and he doesn't have it. I ordered the driver to bring me here," she said and nodded to the side street where the glittering limousine waited.

We waited to hear Pete Plank agree with us but he was next door staring into the shop window.

"Pete," I hissed. "What are you doing?"

"Sorry, Katie. Just looking at all this Spanish gold," he said.

Mabel and Gary looked at me. I looked back at them – one eye on each, which isn't easy – and we all groaned together. "The Coin Collectors' Cabin!"

I cried. "That's what the ram-raiders were aiming for!"

We hopped along to the shop and stared in at the window. Warm, yellow light glinted on a treasure chest that was wrapped in tinsel and overflowed with golden coins. A large sign said...

THE COIN COLLECTORS' CABIN
This week's special offer

REAL
SPANISH PIECES
OF EIGHT

The perfect Christmas gift!

Underneath was a smaller card that explained the golden display.

Collect these wonderful historical Spanish coins – 'pieces of eight' and 'doubloons' – the ones made famous by pirates!

Pieces of eight were made from the silver the Spanish mined in South America and sent back to Spain – if the pirates didn't get them first! They were worth eight 'reales' – about £15 today.

The doubloons were made of gold and the most valuable coins made by the Spanish. Just a handful would have made any pirate a wealthy man.

Did you know... the pieces of eight had a picture of two pillars on one side – the ancient Pillars of Hercules – with a figure eight between them. This 'pillar and eight' mark became the sign for money in some countries. That's why the sign for dollars looks the way it does... $

"This is what the ram-raiders were after!" I said excitedly.

"But they missed and hit the chip shop," Gary nodded.

"Do excuse me, but how could anyone be that stupid?" Mabel asked.

I closed my eyes – well, I closed the one without an eye-patch and I thought about it. "Because they were rotten drivers," I said slowly. "They weren't little robbers – they were kids. Like us. They couldn't drive very well."

"My dad says I'm a great driver," Pete said. "And I'm a kid."

"But you're tall, Pete. And they were so small, they had trouble seeing over the top of the steering-wheel. We've nearly cracked the case! The police are looking for two small robbers – we know we're looking for two kids!"

"Brilliant, Katie!" Pete gasped.

"Yes, brilliant!" came a harsh voice from behind us.

We swung round to see two small figures, dressed in pirate costumes, standing on wooden chair-legs... and pointing plastic pirate pistols at us. One was a boy and one a girl and they both looked exactly the same. Their faces were partly hidden by black beards. "The ram-raiders," I said.

"That's right," the girl said. Suddenly she jumped forward and pointed a pistol at Pete's head. "I'm the famous Mary Read and Darren's the bloodthirsty Blackbeard! This time the big boy drives the car."

I stepped towards them to save my Time Detective pal. The robber boy raised his pistol. "Back off or I fill the big boy full of lead!"

"Do excuse me!" Mabel said. "But the pistols are plastic."

The robber girl shrugged. "Fine. So we'll fill him full of plastic!" She pointed her pistol at Mabel. "You, girl... you came in that posh car. Get the driver over here. We're taking it and big boy here is going to drive it. This time we make no mistakes!"

Mabel said, "Certainly not! Daddy will have the law on you!" So the robbers laughed and dragged Pete towards the mayor's car singing...

"Yo, ho, ho, and a bottle of grog!

Fifteen men on the Dead Man's Dog!"

Chapter 8
The Rolls Royce raiders

The robbers pointed a pistol at the window of the mayor's Rolls Royce car. The mayor's driver jumped out of the car, hands held high and ran off down the street towards the Town Hall. I thought at first he was shouting like a sheep. Then I realised he was shouting, "Mayor! Mayor!"

The raiders tied something to the car aerial. It was a black flag with a skull and crossbones painted in white.

"Interesting," Gary said. "I'll bet you didn't know this! Here's something I copied from *The Bumper Book of Pirates*." He showed me the page...

THE
SKULL AND CROSSBONES

Lots of people believe pirates flew this black flag – but they didn't always! Early pirates flew a plain red flag – when it was flying it meant "No mercy to our victims". Plain black flags meant 'Death'. Later, red or black flags had signs like a bleeding heart, a flaming cannonball, a cutlass or a whole skeleton. Anything to make their victims tremble at the hideous sight.

By about 1730 many pirates were using the skull over crossed bones – an idea they took from the picture often used on gravestones. The nickname of the devil was Old Roger so pirates called their hideous flags "Old Rogers". The name later became "Jolly Roger".

Pirates also collected flags from different countries. So, if they spotted a British ship they flew a British flag and pretended to be friendly. When they got close enough they attacked.

I pulled out Miss Toon's list and scribbled against the note on flags...

and curly wigs

6 wooden legs and eye-patches ✔

7 skull-and-crossbone flags **SOMETIMES**

8 marooning shipmates on

I looked up to see Pete climb into the driver's seat of the Rolls and fasten his seat-belt. The huge car sailed out from the side-street like some great galleon. We stepped back as it rolled down the road towards the shops. When he reached The Coin Collectors' Cabin Pete swung it expertly off the road and sped over the pavement.

We saw a flash of Pete's white face as he fixed his gaze on the treasure chest in the shop window. Then we saw a look of panic in his eye as he struggled with the steering-wheel. The heavy car was beginning to skid on the icy pavement. Instead of racing ahead it was sliding sideways.

"He's not going to make it!" Gary groaned.

The back wheels were spinning and smoking and Mabel was clutching her heart. "Daddy's lovely car!"

There was a cruel crunching crash and the sound of shattering glass as the car smacked into the window of Paddy's Plaice... again.

First came the clattering, chinkling, chunkling fall of breaking glass. There was one tiny moment of silence. Then there were all sorts of noises at once.

A police-car siren sounded far away. A voice cried through the smashed chip shop window, "They're at it again!" Steam hissed from the cracked car radiator.

The car door opened and the radio boomed... Pete Plank staggered from the driver's door and hobbled away from the car. The robbers jumped out and dragged a dazed Pete Plank back. They pulled him, clicking and skidding on their wooden legs, down the street and towards the darkness of the sea-front park. "You are trying to desert our ship!" the girl robber raved. "You know what happens to pirate deserters? Well, that's what you're going to get!"

... and reports are coming in of a plague of chair-leg thefts. Mr Frank Plank of Wexford Way lost one, Mrs Brenda Bucket of Shave Close reported a theft and Mr Clint Grint of Duckpool Drive lost one. Police are puzzled, especially by the report from Mr Albert Dark of Duckpool Park who has actually lost two chair-legs. Crackle... shplizzle... crackle... and we interrupt this report to bring you a news flash. Reports are coming in of a second ram-raid attack on Paddy's Plaice chip shop! Inspector Norse, and his force of course, are rushing to the scene of the crime...

"You see!" Mabel moaned. "If I'd been able to bring my bicycle I'd have caught those rotten robbers! Ooooh!" she ranted and stamped her stump. "They're getting away!"

A police car raced down the street and braked sharply when it reached the chip shop. Unfortunately it hit a patch of ice and shot past like a flea on a ski. Paddy ran to the door of his shop and tried to climb over the bonnet of the Rolls Royce car that was blocking it. His face was red and his hair rising up from his bald skull with rage. He screamed at the police car, "They're here! Arrest these robbers!"

Gary shook his head. "Why is he pointing up the street? Those two ran off down, towards the park."

Mabel prodded him with a sharp finger. "Do excuse me, brainless boy, but the owner of the shop is pointing at us!"

And he was. If he could have got over the bonnet he'd have battered us as flat as fried fishcakes.

"They're dressed as pirates! And I saw three pirates get out of the car!" he was screaming.

"I can explain!" Mabel called to him.

"Don't even try, Mabe babe," Gary said. "Take your leg off and run!"

We took his advice, unstrapped the wooden legs and sprinted down the road, past the reversing police car with the nutty Norse and down to the darkness of the park gates. It was a dead end. We were trapped. The park gates were made of tall iron bars – "Just like the bars we'll be behind for the rest of our lives," Gary groaned.

But I pushed at the gate and it swung open. "The robbers went into the park," I said. "They unlocked the padlock and chain but didn't have time to lock it behind them."

"How did they unlock it?" Gary asked.

"I don't know. But I think it's a clue. Let's go after them."

"It's dark in there," Gary said and his voice was hoarse with fear.

"You're not scared of a little dark, are you Gary?"

"I am!" he whimpered.

"Are you a man or a mouse?" I challenged him.

"Yes!" he replied through trembling teeth.

We wound our way through the twisting paths lit only by the distant lights of the sea-front Christmas illuminations. At last we reached the edge of the pond. The little island was a black shape. Ducks quacked and complained as they waddled over the frozen water. "Do excuse me, you fancy-dressed girl," Mabel said. "But where are we going?"

"Nowhere, fancy-dressed fusspot. We're there," I told her. I turned to Gary. "How did pirates punish their shipmates?"

There was the sound of rusty nails being dragged across wood as Gary scratched his head. "I read it in Captain Johnson's book!" he said. Gary may be a cowardy custard but he is a cowardy custard with a good memory. He said, "A pirate called Captain Roberts made a set of pirate laws called 'The Pirate Articles'..."

The Pirate Articles

1. Every man on the crew has an equal vote on their action and an equal share of food and drink on the ship.
2. All men shall have an equal share of treasure. Any man who takes more than his share of gold or jewels or money shall be punished by marooning.
3. No person shall play cards or dice for money.
4. Lights and candles shall be put out at eight o'clock each night.
5. Each person must make sure his own pistol and cutlass are well kept and ready for use at all times.
6. No boy or woman shall be allowed on board the ship when she sails. Any man carrying a woman to sea shall suffer death
7. Any person who deserts the ship in a battle shall suffer death or marooning.
8. There shall be no fighting on board ship. All quarrels shall be settled on the shore with sword and cutlass
9. No person shall talk of leaving the crew until everyone has shared at least a thousand pounds.
10. The captain shall receive two persons' share of any treasure.
11. The ship's musicians shall be allowed to rest on a Sunday.

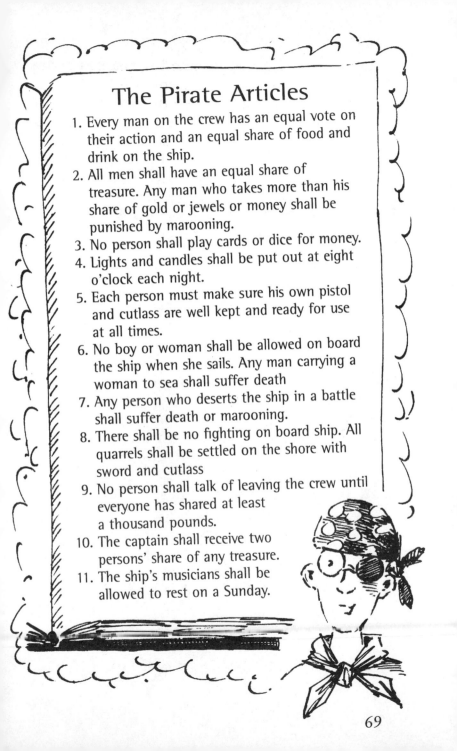

69

In my head I ticked off another couple of Miss Toon's list...

> and curly wigs
>
> 6 wooden legs and eye-patches ✔
>
> 7 skull-and-crossbone flags SOMETIMES
>
> 8 marooning shipmates on desert islands SOMETIMES
>
> ___ the plank ___

"It's rule number seven – 'Any person who deserts the ship in a battle shall suffer death or marooning'," I said. "That's what they accused him of when he climbed out of the crashed car. They said he was a deserter."

"Marooning? Where would they maroon poor Pete?" Gary asked.

"I know where they'd maroon him... and I know who the pirates are, and I know where the treasure's buried," I said. "You've had all the clues, the same as me. Work it out."

Well? Are you as clever as this Time Detective?

Chapter 9
Plank on plank

"Explain what you mean, irritating girl," Mabel said.

I looked over the frozen lake. "Look at the facts:

There are two ram-raiders – a boy and a girl.

The ram-raiders know all about pirates.

The ram-raiders have keys to the park.

The ram-raiders head for the park when they run away.

The park-keeper has twin children, desperate for money.

The park-keeper, Mr Dark, lost two chair-legs earlier this evening.

The ram-raiders hid Mrs Macmanus's purse on an island.

There is an island in the centre of the park lake."

"The park-keeper's twins are the robbers," Gary said slowly. "They got the idea from Miss Toon's project last year. They stole a ship – I mean a car – and tried to attack the Spanish gold. Because they're small they missed – but they took the old lady's purse and buried it on the island in the lake because they didn't want to be caught with £100 in their pockets. But £100 wasn't enough to buy two bikes..."

"So they went back tonight for a second crack at the gold!" Mabel said. "See? I've worked it out!"

"Brilliant, Mabel," I said.

"I know," she said.

"Maybe you can tell us what they've done with Pete?" I said.

"They'll maroon him on the island in the middle of the lake," Mabel added. "They'd leave him with a pistol and some shot to shoot wild animals – that's what pirates did," she said with a smile that glinted red, green and yellow in the lights.

"He won't live long on shot sparrows and ducks – cos that's all there is on that island," I said. "And he'll probably freeze to death on a night like this. We have to rescue him."

"I could call for Daddy's helicopter," Mabel offered.

"No… we'd have to explain everything. We'd have to tell your dad about the pirate costumes and Pete would get into trouble for smashing the car," I said.

"And we'd get into trouble for pinching the chair-legs," Gary sighed.

"I forgot about Daddy!" Mabel cried. "We've only half an hour to get back to the Town Hall before he sits down on his chair!"

"Then let's hurry," I said. "We can't walk across the ice – too dangerous."

"The Dark twins must have done exactly that," Gary said.

"No – they must have used the boats. Look. They're not chained together now! Let's line them up on the ice and use them like a bridge! If the ice cracks the boats will float!"

"Brilliant, Katie!" Gary cried.

"I was going to suggest that," Mabel sniffed.

It took us five desperate minutes to make our bridge and another five to cross it. When we finally stepped ashore, we called, "Pete! Pete! We've come to rescue you!"

And the reply was a cold silence cracked only by the creaking of the ice. "Hah!" Mabel snorted. "So much for your marooning idea! I said they wouldn't leave him here!"

"'They'll maroon him on the island in the middle of the lake', were your exact words, Mabel weedy Tweed," I said angrily.

There were three small trees on the island. It wasn't much bigger than our kitchen. Gary was pacing from one tree to another and counting. "What are you doing?" I asked.

"The treasure map," he said, on his hands and knees and using his chair-leg to grub at the frozen soil. "X marked the spot in the middle and here..." he said, pulling out a bundle of notes, "...is the treasure."

"We'll hand it in and claim the thousand pound reward!" Mabel said. "Let's go!"

"Mabel! We haven't found Gary yet!" I said, waving my chair-leg under her nose.

She sighed. "Pirates didn't draw treasure maps, remember?" she said wearily. "The Dark twins got it wrong. They were hopeless Time Detectives."

"So what if they were?" Gary asked.

"So... I didn't get it wrong about marooning. They got it wrong! They're probably doing something with Pete that pirates never did!"

I snatched her ringlets, pulled her head towards me and kissed her on the forehead. "Do excuse me! But I hope you've washed your mouth!" she grumbled.

"Mabel! Beautiful Mabel! That's the answer!" I cried. "Gary! How did pirates never punish their victims?"

"They never made them walk the plank, Katie," he said.

I scrambled back towards the boat bridge. "Hurry! Before they hurt him!" I called over my shoulder.

"Do excuse me, but where are we going?" Mabel asked.

"Trust me. I know what I'm doing," I said as I jumped ashore and ran towards the sea-front gate of the park.

Chapter 10
Nickers and draws

The sky over the sea front grew brighter as we raced nearer. One black shape stood out against the sky. A tall thin tower with a plank sticking out of the top – the diving board of the swimming-pool.

We skidded to a halt and looked up. A boy wobbled along the plank towards the end while two smaller figures stood at the top of the tower and pointed plastic pistols at him.

"Stop!" I cried. The three figures froze.

"What you want?" the Park Pond Pirate girl called down.

"We want you to bring Pete down safely!" I called back.

"He'll get down safely... when he gets to the end of the plank!" the boy laughed.

"He won't! You'll kill him!" I told them.

"Nah! He can swim! He'll just get a good cold ducking! Serve him right for messing up our raid!" the girl said.

"But the pool's frozen!" I yelled. "He'll smash himself to pieces!"

"You what?"

I picked up a rock from the edge of the path and threw it at the pool. Instead of a splash there was a crunch and the rock slithered over the surface. "Oooops! Sorry!" one of the twins said and began to guide Pete back down to the side of the pool where we were waiting.

"I suppose you'll report us to Inspector Norse," the girl sighed. "We'll hang like all the pirates in history. Darren Dark and Daisy Dark – the famous Park Pond Pirates in prison!"

"Not all pirates were punished," I told her. "Pirates were often pardoned – especially if they gave back their loot."

"Our loot's buried on the island," the boy Darren told me.

"No. It's buried in my pocket. We found it from your map. I'll give it back," I offered.

"Yeah. We never meant to pinch off a poor old woman," Daisy said.

"Do excuse me, but you can't simply say you never meant to do it," Mabel Tweed said sourly. "There is no excuse for theft."

"We just wanted a bike each for Christmas. All the other kids had one, but Dad's too poor," Darren sighed. Mabel opened her mouth to argue but he went on. "You know something? There's even one kid in Duckpool rides around on a golden bike! Doesn't seem fair somehow."

Mabel swallowed. "There are other ways to get a couple of bikes," she said quietly.

"Yeah! Pinch them!" Daisy said sadly.

"No. The Duckpool Council Grand Christmas Raffle has two bikes as prizes," she said.

"Can't afford a ticket," Darren shrugged.

"Well, it so happens that I have a spare one, ticket number 13," Mabel said. "I got it free because my daddy's the mayor, so you can have it. The draw is at eight  o'clock to... aaaagh!" She gave a sudden cry as the distant Town Hall clock began to strike. "Daddy's chair!"

We all knew what she meant. We grabbed the Dark twins and dragged them out of the gates and through the frosty streets. We did our best to explain as we ran. The streets were quiet. Everyone in Duckpool seemed to be in the Town Hall waiting for Mayor Tweed to draw the winning tickets.

We sped up the steps and through the great double doors to the great hall. We pushed through the excited crowds and reached the front as Mayor Tweed was reaching into a drum full of numbered tickets. The crowd went quiet but there was a great rustling of tickets.

The mayor held up a ticket and announced the number. "One hundred and thirty-three."

The crowd rumbled and grumbled. "Shout up, Mayor Tweed!" people called. Mrs Tweed, in her mayoress chain, turned to her husband and said, "Sit down in your mayor's chair and announce it... there's a microphone in front of the chair!"

The man moved to his right, found his chair and sat down heavily.

There was a splintering crash and a cry of pain. The crowd gasped. "The chair-leg nicker's struck again!" they cried in an uproar. Ambulance men pushed their way onto the stage and lifted the moaning mayor onto a stretcher.

Mabel jumped onto the stage and held her father's hand. "Never mind, Daddy! I'll finish tonight's draw!"

"Urrrgh! Gurgle! Gurgle! Urrrgh!" the mayor mumbled.

Mabel turned a dazzling smile on the crowd. "Do excuse me, ladies and gentlemen. But it gives me great pleasure to announce the winner of the two bicycles!"

The mayor's disaster was soon forgotten as the crowd looked at their tickets again. Mabel held up the winning ticket... with her thumb carefully placed over the last figure. "The winner is..." she said into the microphone. "Number... thirteen!"

"We've got it!" the Dark twins screamed. The crowd cheered, some bad losers sighed, and everyone turned to go home. As the great hall emptied we saw Inspector Norse and two constables standing at the door, watching everyone carefully.

"They're looking for the chip-shop raiders – anyone in pirate costume!" I told the others. "We've had it!"

"Leave this to me," Mabel said, and she marched up to the policeman. "Excuse me, police chappie, my good man, but I am Mabel Tweed. My daddy's the mayor, you know. My friends and I have recovered the old lady's money, stolen in the Paddy's Plaice raid." She nodded at me and I handed over the treasure from the Dark twins' hoard.

"Yeah. Well done," he said… but he didn't seem very interested.

"As for our pirate costumes, I can explain," she went on.

"Explain? Explain what, Miss Tweed?" the puzzled policeman said.

"I thought you were looking for pirates!" I told him.

"Nah! That was earlier. Much worse criminals on the loose now. Someone's been going around nicking chair-legs! Nearly killed the mayor – your dad!" he told her.

Mabel looked a little ill. She just nodded to us to slip quietly out of the hall. Pete Plank hung back. "Uhh! Wasn't there a thousand pound reward for finding the treasure?" he asked Inspector Norse.

The policeman blew out his cheeks. "Oh, I suppose there was. Go and see Paddy... though goodness knows who will ever eat a thousand pounds of cod!"

"I think Mabel has a parrot who adores fish," I told the policeman.

"A parrot!!!"

Four Time Detectives, and two Park Pond Pirates with new bikes, set off for Paddy's Plaice and the cod-awful prize.

And, when no-one was looking, six chair-legs were dropped quietly into a Duckpool dustbin.

Time trail

Roman times – even the Romans suffer pirate attacks.
Their great leader, Julius Caesar, is attacked by pirates
and takes a terrible revenge.
Middle Ages – the Vikings are great sailors and will often
attack ships they meet as they travel the seas.

1492   Christopher Columbus discovers America and
claims it for the Spanish. There are vast supplies of
gold and silver in America and the Spanish claim
it for themselves. The trouble is they have to try
and get it back across the Atlantic. That's when
pirates pounce.

1580s   In England Queen Elizabeth is jealous of
Spanish wealth. She puts money towards a
pirate fleet of English sailors led by Francis Drake.
They rob Spanish galleons and land to rob
Spanish gold stores in South America. When
Drake comes back he shares the loot with
Queen Elizabeth.

1660s   Pirates in the Caribbean, known as buccaneers, are making their fortunes, murdering and dying. By 1720 about 2,000 ships are bringing terror to both sides of the Atlantic Ocean. But they are ruining trade so...

1725   Navies set out to drive pirates from the seas. Captain Johnson publishes his famous book on pirates. That's how we know so much about them.

1881   Robert Louis Stevenson writes the famous *Treasure Island* and makes being a pirate seem an exciting life.

1904   Barrie writes *Peter Pan* and pirates become nightmare figures in fancy dress – not much like the real cut-throats who brought terror to sailors.

1990s   Pirates are still roaming the seas, especially in the Far East where there are almost a hundred pirate attacks each year – two every week. Pirates have been around almost as long as ships, and it doesn't look as if they are going to go away.